The Pony-Mad Princess

Princess Ellie's Treasure Hunt

Diana Kimpton

Illustrated by Lizzie Finlay

USBORNE

For Alice and Thomas

This edition first published in 2014 by Usborne Publishing Ltd.,
Usborne House, 83-85 Saffron Hill, London EC1N 8RT, England.
www.usborne.com

First published in 2007 as *Princess Ellie's Secret Treasure Hunt*.
Based on an original concept by Anne Finnis.
Text copyright © 2007 by Diana Kimpton and Anne Finnis.
Illustrations copyright © 2007 by Lizzie Finlay.

A CIP catalogue record for this book is available from the British Library.

ISBN 9781409566076 JFMAM JASOND/14   01434/2

Printed in Chatham, Kent, UK.

The Pony-Mad Princess

Princess Ellie's Treasure Hunt

The paper wasn't blank. There was old-fashioned writing on it that was hard to read. There were squiggly lines too and drawings of trees. Ellie's hands shook with excitement as she unrolled the last part of the scroll. The writing at the top was in capital letters. They spelled out a single word.

"Treasure!" cried Ellie, Kate and

04336387

Look out for more sparkly adventures of

The Pony-Mad Princess!

Chapter 1

"Can I stop now?" asked Princess Ellie.

"Certainly not," replied Miss Stringle. "Your holiday does not begin until your lessons are over, and there is still half an hour to go."

"But John will be here soon," pleaded Ellie.

"No, he won't," said her teacher, firmly.

The Pony-Mad Princess

"Prince John is not due to arrive for another hour. Now please get on with your work. Princesses should not argue."

Ellie sighed. She was tired of her history lesson. She was tired of studying in the palace library, and she was tired of its rows of old books stored in ancient bookcases. She longed to be out in the sunshine with her ponies. Perhaps Miss Stringle would change her mind once she'd finished the worksheet.

The long list of questions was all about princesses from the past. She'd been working on them all afternoon. Thank goodness there were only three left.

She chewed the end of her pencil as she turned the gold-edged pages of *The Complete Guide to the Royal Family*.

Princess Ellie's Treasure Hunt

The huge book was packed with boring information. It said when people were born and when they died, but it never mentioned whether they liked ponies as much as Ellie did.

She quickly discovered that Princess Marissa's older brother was called James and that Princess Andromeda had married King Proctor the Proud of Protavia. It took her much longer to work out that Princess Traviata was her great-great-great-great-aunt.

She wrote down the last answer and waved her paper in the air. "I've finished," she declared. "Can I stop now?"

The Pony-Mad Princess

"Not quite yet," replied her teacher. She pointed at the books spread out in front of Ellie. "I want you to put those back in their right places while I mark your work. Then I can see if you've remembered what I taught you about how the library is organized."

Ellie groaned. She hadn't listened to Miss Stringle droning on and on about the library. She'd been far too busy daydreaming about her five beautiful ponies. Now she had no idea where the books belonged.

She stacked them on top of each other, picked them up and set off round the room. As she walked, she looked at the shelves carefully, searching for spaces that might give her a clue.

The first gap she spotted was high above

8

her head. As she stood on tiptoe to push
a book into it, the rest of the pile wobbled.

She tried to steady it, and she almost
succeeded. But one book slid off. It tumbled

to the ground, slid across the shiny wooden floor and vanished under a bookcase.

Luckily, Miss Stringle didn't notice. She was still busy with her marking. So Ellie dumped the other books on a table. Then she lay down and looked under the nearest set of shelves.

The book was right at the back, resting against the wall. She reached out to grab it and felt something long and soft brush against her fingers.

Ellie pulled her hand away in surprise. Then she peered under the bookcase again and spotted a piece of red ribbon dangling from the back of the bottom shelf. "I wonder how long that's been there," she thought. The maids would never have noticed it while they were sweeping.

Princess Ellie's Treasure Hunt

This was much more interesting than her lesson. She forgot about the book for a moment and pulled gently on the ribbon. It didn't move. She pulled again a bit harder. This time it shifted a little and then got stuck.

Ellie gave it a short, sharp tug and the ribbon finally pulled free. As it slid out of its hiding place, she saw for the first time that it was tied round a tightly rolled scroll of paper.

"Princess Aurelia!" shouted Miss Stringle. "Get up at once. Princesses do not grovel on the floor."

"I'm sorry," said Ellie, wishing her teacher wouldn't use her real name. "I was just fetching a book I dropped." She decided not to mention the scroll. That was her secret, and she wasn't ready to share it yet.

Chapter 2

Ellie grabbed hold of the book with one hand and the scroll with the other. Then she stood up very carefully, turning to face Miss Stringle at the same time. She held the book in front of her to attract her teacher's attention and kept the paper hidden safely behind her back. If Miss Stringle didn't know it existed, she couldn't

Princess Ellie's Treasure Hunt

take it away or make Ellie write about it.

Keeping her eyes fixed on her teacher, Ellie stepped sideways towards the table. Miss Stringle watched her curiously. "Why are you moving in such a peculiar way?" she asked.

The Pony-Mad Princess

Ellie's mind raced, searching for a remotely believable reply. But before she could think of one, there was a loud knock on the library door. Miss Stringle looked round to see who was there, and Ellie quickly slid the scroll up inside her sleeve without being spotted. She would have to wait until later to discover what was written on it.

Higginbottom, the butler, stepped into the library and gave a low bow. "I'm sorry to interrupt," he said, "but Prince John of Andirovia has arrived earlier than expected. He's waiting for Princess Aurelia to welcome him."

Ellie gave a whoop of delight. Although she emailed John all the time, she hadn't seen him since the royal visit to his parents' palace. "Can I stop now?" she asked for the

third time. "Princesses should be polite
to guests."

"That's true," agreed Miss Stringle, with a
sigh. "I suppose you'd better go. And don't
forget to have a good holiday."

"I won't," cried Ellie, as she rushed out of
the library. She expected to find her friend
waiting for her outside. But he wasn't there.
The corridor was empty.

The butler winked at her
and smiled. "Prince John
thought you'd like him to get
you out of class," he explained.
"He's gone straight to the
blue guest room to
change into his riding
clothes. He'll meet
you at the stables."

The Pony-Mad Princess

"Brilliant," said Ellie. John was as pony-mad as she was. It was going to be wonderful having him to stay for the whole holiday.

She raced up the spiral stairs to her very pink bedroom, took off her frilly, pink dress and put on her pink jodhpurs. As she slid her feet into her new, pink riding boots, she remembered the scroll. She hadn't wanted to tell Miss Stringle about it, but her friends were different. It would be fun to share the secret with them.

She picked up her dress from the floor and pulled the roll of paper out of its sleeve. She stared at it for a moment, wondering what was written inside. Then she ran down to the stables to meet John, clutching the scroll safely in her hand.

When she reached the yard, she found her

other friend was already there. Kate, the cook's granddaughter, was home early from school, and she was busy grooming her brown and white foal, Angel.

Before they had time to speak, John ran into the yard carrying a long cardboard box. "Look at this!" he cried, as he waved the box at the two girls. "It's my latest gadget. I only got it this morning, so I couldn't resist bringing it with me." He kneeled down and started pulling off the sticky tape that held the box shut.

Ellie was too excited about her own news to wait for him. "I've got something to show you too. But it's a secret. You've got to promise not to tell." She waited impatiently until the others had agreed. Then she held out the scroll and explained, "I found this during my history lesson. It was hidden behind the books in the library."

"It looks really old," said Kate. "The ribbon's faded."

"And the paper's yellow with age," said Ellie.

"Old things aren't always interesting," said John. "It might be a blank piece of paper or a shopping list."

For a second or two, his words made Ellie doubt her own enthusiasm. Then she realized he must be wrong. "No one would hide a shopping list," she declared. She pulled the ribbon undone. Then she carefully started to unroll the scroll, holding it out so the others could see it.

The paper wasn't blank. There was old-fashioned writing on it that was hard to read. There were squiggly lines too and drawings of trees.

"It's a map!" cried John. "Those squiggles mean a stream and those two lines over there mean a bridge."

Kate pointed at a large cross. "It's telling us where to find something. But what?"

Ellie's hands shook with excitement as she unrolled the last part of the scroll. The writing at the top was in capital letters. They spelled out a single word.

"Treasure!" cried Ellie, Kate and John together.

Chapter 3

"Wow!" said John. "I've never seen a real treasure map before."

"Look at the date!" cried Kate. "It's a hundred years old."

"That's even older than Great-Aunt Edwina," laughed Ellie. She peered at the strange writing and started to read it out. "Go to the place north of the stream where three oak trees grow. Start by the tree that's closest to the palace. Walk ten paces towards the west and start to dig. My treasure is hidden under the ground."

"That's brilliant," said John. "Now you've *got* to be interested in my gadget. It's just what we need." He ripped open the box and pulled out a metal circle attached to a long handle.

"That's a funny-shaped spade," laughed Kate. John gave a superior smile. "It's not a spade. It's a metal detector. It will help us find exactly the right place to dig."

Princess Ellie's Treasure Hunt

"It won't if the treasure's not metal," said Kate.

"But it will be," John insisted. "We're so near to the sea that it must be pirates' treasure and pirates always bury gold!"

"I'm not so sure," said Ellie. "It could have been buried by a princess who wanted to hide all her rubies and diamonds and emeralds."

"Or it could be masses and masses of paper money buried by a millionaire," suggested Kate.

"Bother!" sighed John, his voice tinged with disappointment. "My metal detector's not going to find any of those things." Then he thought for a moment and grinned. "But it will find the treasure chest. Treasure chests always have metal hinges."

At that moment, Angel nudged John's arm so hard that he nearly dropped his new gadget. Then she started to paw the ground with one of her front hooves.

Kate laughed. "She's tired of standing still. She's not as excited by treasure as we are."

"Shadow would be if it was peppermints," said Ellie. They were her Shetland pony's favourite sweets.

John patted the foal's neck. "She's grown since I last saw her. Is she big enough to ride yet?"

"No," said Kate. "It will be ages before she's strong enough. She's still only a baby."

"And she still stays close to her mum," added Ellie. "She likes to follow behind if one of us is riding Starlight."

At the mention of her name, a bay mare

put her head over the nearest stable door and whickered gently. Angel whickered back and reached out her nose to nuzzle her mother.

"Let's go for a ride with them now," suggested John. "We could try to find those oak trees."

"Which trees?" asked Meg, the palace groom, as she carried a bulging haynet into the yard.

Ellie hesitated. She wanted to keep the map secret so she could find the treasure

with her friends. She didn't want her parents to take over and make Higginbottom dig the hole for her with a silver spade. But she hated the idea of lying to Meg.

Luckily, John was good at talking his way out of problems. "I meant the trees on the drawing Ellie found in the library," he said. It was the perfect reply. It gave just enough information, but not too much.

Ellie followed his lead. "We're going to look for the place it shows."

"And we're going to take Starlight and Angel," added Kate.

"Have a lovely time," said Meg. "But go steadily and stay out of the woods. Foals can be silly. They're not good at keeping out of danger."

It didn't take them long to decide which of Ellie's five ponies they would ride. Kate wanted Starlight so she could be close to Angel. John chose Sundance, the chestnut, because he was the same colour as John's own two ponies at home. The final decision was Ellie's and she picked Rainbow, her grey Welsh pony.

They put on the ponies' saddles and bridles and rode out of the yard towards the deer park. As they went up the lane, they chatted excitedly about the treasure. There were so many things it could be and so many people who could have buried it. But John was still convinced that it was pirates' gold.

At first, Angel kept close to Starlight. Then they passed the paddock where Ellie's other two ponies were enjoying a rest. Shadow was busy eating as usual. But Moonbeam, the palomino, cantered towards them and stood with her head over the fence.

Angel couldn't resist saying "hello". She trotted over to her friend and sniffed noses. Starlight whinnied after her, obviously worried that her baby had gone too far away. Angel whinnied a reply and trotted back to join her.

As soon as they reached the deer park, the ponies started to jog and pull on their reins. They could feel the grass beneath their feet and wanted to go faster. Ellie knew they needed to use up some energy, but she remembered Meg's warning. "We'd better not gallop with Angel," she said to the others. "Let's have a canter instead."

She let the grey pony trot for a few steps. Then she sat down in the saddle and squeezed her legs against Rainbow's sides. The pony obediently broke into a steady canter – not too fast and not too slow. Ellie relaxed in the saddle – cantering was so comfortable. It always reminded her of riding her old rocking horse.

Kate and John rode beside her, matching Rainbow's speed. Angel kept up easily. Her legs were thin and spindly, but they were nearly as long as Starlight's. She was obviously enjoying herself. She tossed her head with delight as her hooves pounded across the grass.

They cantered across the corner of the deer park towards the stream. When they were nearly there, they slowed the ponies to a walk. "Let's look for those trees," said Ellie.

"There's a weeping willow over there," said Kate, pointing at a large tree on the opposite bank. Its branches drooped down into the water.

"That's no good," said John. "It's on the wrong side of the stream and it's the wrong sort of tree. We're only interested in oaks."

"There aren't any here," said Ellie. The banks of the stream were covered with grass and wild flowers. The willow was the only tree close to the water.

"The ones on the map were further away from the stream," said John. "We'd better investigate those over there." He waved his arm towards several groups of trees that dotted the open parkland.

As they walked the ponies towards the closest group, Starlight whinnied again. Angel had got left behind. She was busy sniffing the bushes and tasting the wild flowers.

The foal squealed in response to her mum's call and cantered over to her. But she didn't stop. She sped on, lifting her back legs as she went in a playful buck. She reached the trees, then spun round and galloped back.

"She's not keeping as close to her mum as I'd expected," said John.

Ellie watched anxiously as Angel galloped away again. "She's getting more confident all the time," she said. "She didn't run around like this last time we took her out."

"I wish she wasn't doing it today," said Kate, as the foal hurtled in between the trees. "Where's she gone now?"

Starlight whinnied for her again and again, but this time there was no reply. Angel had completely disappeared.

Chapter 4

"Oh, no," said Ellie. "Meg told us to keep Angel out of the woods."

"It's not really a wood," said John. "It's just a few trees growing close together." But he looked as worried as the others.

They trotted over to where they had last seen the foal. Ellie's stomach was knotted with nerves. Suppose Angel was hurt?

Her spindly legs could break so easily.

Suddenly there was a loud crashing in the undergrowth, and the brown and white foal raced out in front of them. Rainbow was so surprised that she jumped sideways. But Ellie didn't mind. She was just pleased to see that Angel was all right. "I think we should keep away from the trees now," she said.

"I think so too," agreed Kate. "It's not a safe place for a foal."

"But we need to look at them if we're going to find the treasure," said John. "I'm dying to find out what it is."

"Angel's more important than that," said Ellie, firmly. "We'll have to come back tomorrow without her." She turned Rainbow round and headed back towards the stables.

Princess Ellie's Treasure Hunt

Kate and John turned Starlight and Sundance too, and Angel followed them. As they rode, John looked up at the sky. "Would your dad lend us a helicopter?" he asked. "My parents have three and they  are always happy to let me use one."

Ellie sighed. John was very good at persuading the Emperor and Empress of Andirovia to let him have his own way. She had much more trouble with the King and Queen. "Dad's only got one," she admitted. "And he's not likely to let us have that. He uses it too much himself."

"Anyway, we'd have to tell him why we wanted it," added Kate. "I thought this was supposed to be a secret so we can look for the treasure by ourselves."

"It is," said John. "But it would be so much easier to spot the right trees from the air. Then we could see everything laid out just like it is on the map."

To Ellie's relief, they managed to get back to the stables without losing Angel again. The foal still wandered off from time to time when she saw something interesting to explore. But there were no trees here so she never went out of sight.

Just as they reached the yard, Ellie had an idea. "There is another way to get up high," she said, pointing at the palace. "The towers are really tall. We'll get a fantastic view of the grounds if we climb up to the top of one."

"Brilliant," said Kate.

John grinned. "We'll have time to do it before tea if we hurry."

They unsaddled the ponies as quickly as they could and settled them in their stables with fresh water and plenty of hay. Then they ran back to their rooms to get changed out of their riding clothes before they went exploring.

Ten minutes later, they met at the bottom of the West Tower. Ellie was the last to arrive. She found the others sitting on the stairs waiting for her. "Sorry I'm late," she said. "I went back for my binoculars."

"I've brought mine too," said John, holding up a much bigger pair. "They're explorer grade with digital focusing, tinted lenses and—"

"Tell us later," interrupted Ellie. "We need to get started. It's an awful long way to the top."

The spiral stairs were covered with soft, red carpet that muffled the sound of their footsteps. The walls were lined with paintings of Ellie's relatives.

Kate looked at the pictures anxiously as she climbed the steps. "I wish their eyes weren't following me," she said.

"They're not. It's just an optical illusion," said John. He stopped to look at a painting of a man in old-fashioned clothes who was holding an elaborate brass object with lots of knobs. "Wow! Look at that gadget! I wish I had one like that."

"And I'd love a tiara with golden horseshoes on it just like hers," said Ellie, pointing at a picture of a girl and a boy dressed in royal clothes.

"I wonder if she's one of the princesses I was learning about today. Princess Marissa had a brother."

"Whoever she was, I think she was as pony-mad as us," laughed Kate. She climbed another step and stared at a painting of a man on a horse. "Tiaras aren't really my thing. I'd much rather have a white stallion like his."

"He'd be too big for you," said John. "You'll have to wait until you're grown-up."

"When I grow up, I'm going to have my own stables," said Kate.

"I'm going to have seven horses," said John. "One for each day of the week."

"And I'm going to put a lift in this tower," added Ellie. "My legs are aching."

The higher they climbed, the steeper

the stairs became. The carpet stopped at the fourth floor. After that, the steps were bare wood and the handrail was a piece of rope screwed to the wall.

Ellie held the rope tightly as she climbed up and up. She hoped desperately that her plan was going to work. All this effort would be worthwhile if it helped them find the treasure. But it would be dreadful if they couldn't spot the right trees when they reached the top.

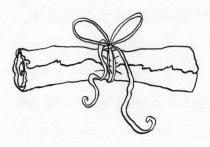

Chapter 5

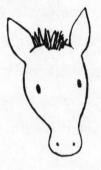

At long last, Ellie and her friends reached the top of the stairs and stepped out into a circular room with brick walls. They paused for a moment to get their breath back. Then they ran over to the only window and peered out.

Ellie was right. The view was fantastic. They could see the palace grounds spread out beneath them.

Princess Ellie's Treasure Hunt

"Look how blue the sea is," said John, pointing at the distant horizon.

"And look at all those trees," groaned Kate. "How are we going to tell which are the ones near the treasure?"

"The map will help," said Ellie. She spread it out on the window sill for them all to see.

"There's the stream," said John, pointing at the wiggly lines on the paper.

"And there it is outside," said Kate. "You can see the sun glinting on the water."

John looked at the map again. "It doesn't show the whole stream. Just the bit near the bridge. So that's the next thing we've got to find."

"Which bridge?" asked Kate. "There are two of them."

"Bother!" said John. "I can't tell which one it is on the map."

"But I know," said Ellie. "One of them's quite new. I had to cut the ribbon at the opening ceremony when I was four. So it wasn't here a hundred years ago."

"Where's the one that was?" asked John.

It took Ellie a little while to spot it. "It's

Princess Ellie's Treasure Hunt

over there," she shouted, as she pointed out of the window. "Now let's find those trees."

Ellie peered through her binoculars, looking carefully at the groups of trees that dotted the palace grounds. From her high viewpoint, she soon realized that several of the groups were too big. They contained far too many trees. Some of the others weren't close enough to the stream.

"Those might be the ones," she said, pointing at a group of trees not far from the bridge.

"And so could those over there," said John, pointing at another group. "But I think those are the only two groups of trees that might be the ones on the map."

"So do I," said Ellie. "The treasure must be beside one of them." A shiver of excitement ran down her spine as she gazed out of the window. "It's just sitting there under the ground, waiting for us to find it."

"I wish we could look for it now," cried Kate.

"So do I," said John.

"But we can't," sighed Ellie. "We'll get into trouble if we're late for tea, and we've still got to go down all those stairs again."

*

Princess Ellie's Treasure Hunt

They met at the stables the next morning,
straight after breakfast. Ellie had the map.
Kate had two spades that she'd borrowed
from her grandfather and John had his
metal detector.

"It's a good thing it's got a super deluxe
folding handle," he said. "Otherwise it
wouldn't fit in my backpack."

"I wish the spades had
them too," groaned
Kate. "Their handles
stick out the top of
my backpack."

They groomed the
ponies quickly and put on
their saddles and bridles. Then they
mounted and set off towards the stream.
Ellie led the way on Rainbow. John was

riding Sundance again, but Kate had Moonbeam this time. They'd decided it was safer to leave Starlight at home with Angel.

The first group of trees they reached was the one by the bend in the stream. As soon as they arrived, John jumped down from his saddle and started to unpack his metal detector.

There were three trees, just like on the map, and they were all enormous. Ellie rode Rainbow in amongst them and stared up at the mass of green leaves that shut out the sun. Then she noticed something.

"We're in the wrong place," she shouted to the others. "These aren't oaks."

"How do you know?" said John, as he unfolded the super deluxe handle. "They're big enough to be oaks."

Princess Ellie's Treasure Hunt

"But they've got the wrong sort of
leaves," said Ellie.

Kate rode up beside her and looked
carefully at the trees. "Ellie's right," she
agreed. "Oak leaves have wigglier edges.
I learned about them at school."

"Come on," said Ellie. "Let's try the other place."

John looked longingly at his metal detector. "Perhaps I should have a practice while we're here," he suggested.

"No!" shouted Ellie and Kate together.

John sighed and put the gadget back in his pack. Then he swung himself into Sundance's saddle and they rode on towards the other trees they'd spotted from the tower.

Ellie's stomach was churning with nerves. Surely this must be the right place. If it wasn't, there was nowhere else to look and they'd never find the treasure.

Chapter 6

As soon as Ellie, Kate and John arrived at the other group of trees, they saw there were three huge oaks. But they weren't alone. There were several smaller trees growing around them.

"Does that mean we're in the wrong place again?" asked Kate. "The map doesn't say anything about other trees."

"But the map was drawn a hundred years ago," said John. "Those smaller trees are much younger than that. They wouldn't have been here then."

Ellie grinned. "Let's get started," she said. "I want to find that treasure."

They tied the ponies to the trees with the headcollars they'd brought with them. Then Ellie pulled out the map and looked at the instructions again.

"We've got to start by the oak closest to the palace," she said.

"That's that one over there," said Kate.

They walked over to it and squeezed through the brambles

52

and bracken to reach the trunk. "Now take ten paces to the west," read Ellie.

"Wait a minute," said John. He rummaged in his backpack and pulled out a small, black gadget. "It's my new explorer-grade compass. It tells you the time, the date and your height above sea level."

"But does it tell you which way's west?" asked Kate.

"Of course it does," replied John. He looked at the gadget. Then he pointed into the distance and said, "It's that way."

"Great," said Ellie. "Now, all together. Ten paces forwards."

"One, two, three…" they counted as they slowly stepped forward in the direction John had pointed. But when they reached "ten", they found they weren't all in the same place. Kate was furthest back, Ellie was a little way ahead of her and John was well out in front.

"Bother," said Ellie. "We've all taken different-sized steps. How can we know which of us is right?"

"John's definitely wrong," said Kate. "He took ridiculously big steps."

Princess Ellie's Treasure Hunt

John folded his arms and sighed. "That's because I was pretending to be a pirate. Pirates always have long legs."

"Short pirates don't," argued Kate. "The only thing pirates always have is a parrot."

"It doesn't matter anyway," said Ellie. "We don't know for sure that this is pirates' treasure. It could have been buried by someone else."

"Someone who takes small steps like me," said Kate.

"Or someone who takes big steps like mine," said John.

"Or any size steps in between," said Ellie. "The treasure could be hidden anywhere between the two of you."

John grinned. "Now you know why we need my metal detector. Let's put sticks in the ground to show where each of us ended up. Then I'll know where to search."

He pulled the gadget out of his backpack and unfolded the super deluxe handle. Then he started to swing the metal detector slowly from side to side, keeping the bottom of it close to the ground.

Ellie and Kate watched anxiously. They didn't have to wait long. After only a few seconds, the machine started to bleep loudly.

John pointed triumphantly at the ring on bottom of the metal detector. "I've found it," he yelled. "The treasure's under here."

Ellie and Kate grabbed the spades and started to dig. Luckily, the ground was quite soft, but digging was still hard work. There were so many roots in the way. Suddenly, Ellie's spade clinked against something hard.

Princess Ellie's Treasure Hunt

"There's something here!" she yelled.
She kneeled down and scrabbled in the
soil with her fingers. But all she found was
an old, metal bottle top. "That's not it,"
she said, as she threw it to one side in
disgust.

John waved the metal detector over it.
The machine bleeped in exactly the same
way it had before. Then he waved it over
the hole and there was a horrible silence.

"Sorry," he said, as his ears turned pink with embarrassment. "False alarm. There's nothing else there."

He started to search again, walking slowly back towards the oaks. For a long time, he worked in silence. Then the metal detector bleeped again.

Princess Ellie's Treasure Hunt

"I hope this really is the treasure," said Ellie, as she and Kate started to dig again. But it wasn't. This time all they found was a rusty nail.

Kate gave an exaggerated yawn. "That's even less exciting than the bottle top."

"No, it's not," said John, looking at it carefully. "This isn't any old nail. It's a nail from a horseshoe. You can tell by its shape."

"But it's still not treasure," said Ellie.

"I'm sure we'll find the real thing soon," said John, as he started to search again. But he sounded slightly less confident than he had before.

"I hope we won't have to dig too many holes," said Kate. "I'm getting tired."

"So am I," said Ellie. "Let's have a rest."

They wandered back to the copse and

checked that the ponies were all right.
Then they sat down on a tree stump and
watched John waving the metal detector
around.

After a while, Ellie got bored and looked
round at where she was sitting. There were
some leafy twigs sticking out from the side
of the stump. What was left of the tree was
trying to grow again.

Princess Ellie's Treasure Hunt

Ellie stared at the twigs in alarm. Then she nudged Kate with her elbow. "What kind of leaves are they?" she asked, pointing at the twigs.

"Oak, I think," replied Kate.

"I think so too," sighed Ellie. She jumped to her feet and looked closely at the stump. "This tree had a much wider trunk than the other oaks, so it must have been older than them. That means there were four oaks here one hundred years ago, not three."

Kate's shoulders slumped in despair. "No wonder we haven't found the treasure. We're in the wrong place."

"But there's nowhere else to look," groaned Ellie. "We've no chance of finding the treasure now."

Chapter 7

They took the long way home to cheer themselves up. It was fun jumping over logs in the woods and galloping through the deer park. But it didn't take away their disappointment.

"Are you sure there's nowhere else to look?" asked Kate, as they clattered into the yard.

"Definitely," said John. He jumped down from Sundance's back and patted the chestnut pony's neck. "Those were the only groups of trees in the right place. The map must be talking about a different palace."

Ellie thoughtfully twisted a strand of Rainbow's mane round her fingers. "It doesn't make sense. Why would anyone hide a map of somewhere else in our library?"

John and Kate both shrugged their shoulders. None of them knew the answer to that question. All they knew was that they'd failed. The excitement of the treasure hunt was over.

They unsaddled the ponies and turned them loose in the paddock with Starlight and Angel. Then they hung the headcollars up in the tack room and walked miserably out of the yard. There was no point in wondering what kind of treasure it was now. It didn't matter any more. They weren't going to find it.

They were halfway back to the palace when they met an old lady in a long skirt. "Deary me!" she said. "I'm sure children didn't look that gloomy when I was a girl."

The sight of her favourite great-aunt cheered Ellie up a little. She smiled weakly and said, "I didn't know you were coming."

"Neither did I until this morning," replied Great-Aunt Edwina. "That's when I decided

I couldn't stand the muddle at home any longer. The builders have made such a mess. There's dust everywhere and muddy footprints all over the floor."

Ellie's eyes glinted with mischief. "I suppose it was never like that when you were a girl," she said, echoing her great-aunt's favourite complaint.

Great-Aunt Edwina burst out laughing. "Actually it was much worse then. You should have seen all the mess here when your great-grandfather landscaped the palace grounds. The whole place looked like a building site."

"I wish I'd seen it," said John. "I like bulldozers and diggers and cranes."

"I'm not sure they had all of those," said the old lady. "But they had lots of men with shovels. They laid the gravel drive, dug the fish pond, moved the bridge and built the wall around the kitchen garden."

Ellie, Kate and John stared at her, open-mouthed with astonishment. Kate was the first to recover enough to speak. "Did you say they moved the bridge?"

"Yes, my dear," said Great-Aunt Edwina.

"So a hundred years ago, it must have been in a different place," said Ellie. Her disappointment had been replaced by a glimmer of hope.

"Of course it was," replied Great-Aunt Edwina.

"Where?" asked Ellie, Kate and John together.

The old lady gazed thoughtfully at the sky as if she expected to find the answer written on it. "I think it was further west," she said. Then she looked doubtful and added, "Or was it further east?"

"Can't you remember?" pleaded Kate.

The old lady shook her head sadly. "I'm afraid not. My memory is not as good as it was when I was a girl." Then she looked at her watch and tut-tutted to herself. "Now I'll have to say goodbye. I've arranged for Higginbottom to bring me tea and cakes on the lawn." She turned and walked away towards the palace garden.

Ellie waited until she was out of earshot. Then she said, "It's a good thing she didn't ask why we were so interested in the bridge."

"But it's a shame she couldn't tell us where it was," grumbled John.

The Pony-Mad Princess

Kate nodded. "I wonder how we can we find out?" she asked.

Suddenly, a pony started to whinny loudly. It wasn't a happy sound. It had an edge of fear. A shiver ran down Ellie's back as she realized she'd heard it before on yesterday's ride. "It's Starlight!" she yelled, as she ran towards the paddock. "There's something wrong with Angel."

Princess Ellie's Treasure Hunt

Kate's face was white as she raced beside Ellie. John was close behind them and, in the distance, Ellie could see Meg running from the stables. She must have heard Starlight too.

They found the bay mare on the far side of the paddock. She was cantering up and down the fence, calling loudly for her baby. Sundance, Rainbow and Moonbeam were watching her. But there was no sign of Angel.

"She must have got out," said Meg. "But I don't see how. I checked the fence myself this morning."

"Perhaps she crawled underneath," suggested John.

Kate shook her head and sniffed back a tear. "I don't think she could. The bottom rail's too low."

The Pony-Mad Princess

Suddenly, Ellie noticed that one of the fence posts was leaning over slightly. It was standing next to a tree and between the two was a tiny gap. Ellie pointed at it and asked, "Could Angel have got through there?"

Meg ran over and examined the spot. "The little rascal's pushed the post over with her bottom," she said, pointing at some strands of brown and white hair caught in the wood. "The space is just big enough for her to wriggle through. But it's too small for Starlight to follow."

Kate stared anxiously over the fence. "She could be anywhere in the grounds by now."

"Don't worry," said Ellie. "We'll find her." But deep inside, she didn't feel as confident as she sounded. Perhaps the foal's curiosity had got her into real trouble this time.

Chapter 8

John squeezed through the gap in the fence and looked carefully at the ground. Then he shook his head. "I can't see any hoofprints. They don't show up on this springy grass."

"Oh, no," groaned Kate. "That means we've no idea which way she went."

"But we know she's not anywhere we can see," said Ellie. "That rules out all the open grassland. It would be easy to spot her there."

"We'd better split up and start searching," said Meg. "You come with me, Kate. We'll look down towards the stream. Ellie, you go with John and search further north."

Ellie wriggled through the gap and raced off with John in the direction Meg had pointed. There were several clumps of trees over there. Perhaps Angel was hiding in one of them.

The first group of trees was small. It was easy to see that Angel wasn't there. The second was much bigger. They had to go in between the trees to check. The leafy branches met above their heads, shutting out the sunlight. Elle was thankful that Angel wasn't brown all over. It should be easy to spot her white patches in the gloom.

Minutes ticked by while they searched every possible place she could be. "She's not here," said John at last.

"We'd better try somewhere else," said Ellie. She ran out into the sunlight again and headed for the next group of trees. "Angel," she called as she ran up to it. "Where are you, Angel?"

To her delight, she heard a faint whinny in response. John heard it too. They both stopped, hoping the foal would run out and surprise them like she had the previous day.

But she didn't. She just whinnied again, louder this time and more urgently. "She's frightened," said Ellie, as she ran in amongst the trees. John raced close beside her.

They had to force their way through the

The Pony-Mad Princess

thick undergrowth between the trees.
Prickles tugged at their clothes and tore their
hands. But Ellie didn't care. Saving Angel
was worth a few scratches.

They found the foal trapped in a dense
patch of brambles. The strong stems were
wound round her legs. Her neck was damp
with sweat from her efforts to free herself.

But the more she struggled, the more entangled she became.

"You're all right now," said Ellie in a soothing voice. "We'll soon get you out of there." She bent down and tugged hard on one of the stems, trying to pull it away from Angel.

The foal flinched and squealed with pain. A trickle of blood ran down her leg where a sharp thorn had dug into her skin.

"I'm sorry," said Ellie, fighting back the tears that filled her eyes. The last thing she'd wanted to do was hurt Angel even more.

"We can't pull the brambles off," said John. "We'll have to cut her free."

Ellie cheered up. "Go on then," she said. "You must have a knife in your survival kit."

"Of course I have," said John. "It's an explorer-grade camping knife with twenty-four different functions." Then his ears turned pink again. "Trouble is, I didn't bring it with me. It's back at the stables in my backpack."

Ellie groaned. There was nothing else they could do by themselves. "We've got to fetch help," she said. "But we can't leave Angel here on her own. She might panic."

"I'll go," said John. "You stay behind. Angel knows you better than me." He spun round and raced off towards the stables.

The foal snorted with alarm at the sudden movement. She started to struggle again, trying to pull herself free from the brambles. Ellie knew she had to stop her. If she didn't, Angel might snap one of her spindly legs.

Chapter 9

"Steady, Angel," said Ellie, trying hard not to let her own fear show. "You've got to stand still or you might hurt yourself really badly."

To Ellie's relief, the sound of her voice made the foal relax. Angel flicked her ears forward and stopped struggling against the brambles. But as soon as Ellie stopped speaking, the frightened foal resumed her fight to get free.

So Ellie started talking again, saying the first thing that came into her head. She told Angel how beautiful she was and how John would be back soon with help to cut her free. She told her about the treasure and how they didn't know where to look for it. And all the time she was speaking, the foal stood still and listened.

It didn't matter what Ellie said. It was the sound of the words that mattered – not their meaning. She rambled on and on. When she started to run out of things to say, she looked round her for inspiration.

"That's an oak tree over there," she said. "You can tell because the leaves have wiggly edges. That's another oak over there and that other tree's an oak too.

Princess Ellie's Treasure Hunt

"Look how big they are," she continued, as she glanced round to make sure there weren't any more. "They're much older than you. They must have been here for years and years and years."

She paused and licked her lips. They were dry from so much talking. But Angel didn't like the silence. She snorted and started to struggle again.

"Please don't do that," said Ellie, stroking the foal's face. "I promise I won't stop again." As she spoke she looked out through the trees at the open ground in front of them. She could see Kate, John and Meg running across the grass. Help was nearly here, but she knew she had to keep talking until it arrived.

"The stream's right over there, Angel. But we can't see the bridge. That's too far away." As she was speaking, she spotted two identical mounds close together on the bank of the stream. "Look at those," she told Angel. "They're much too square to be natural. And there are matching mounds on the opposite bank. I bet they're all that's left of the old bridge."

At that moment, John raced up with Kate and Meg close behind. "I've brought my knife this time," he said, as he pulled it out of his backpack."

"And Meg's borrowed pruners from the gardener," said Kate. She patted Angel's neck and slipped a headcollar over her brown and white nose. "I'm not going to let you run away again," she told the pony, as she fastened the strap behind Angel's ears.

"We've got to keep talking," explained Ellie. "It keeps her calm."

So they chattered about what they were doing as they worked to free the trapped foal. First Meg and John cut through the twisting stems. Then Kate and Ellie helped them pull the vicious thorns away from Angel's legs and body. Soon their own hands and arms were covered with scratches, but nobody complained.

When the foal was finally free, Meg ran her fingers over Angel's legs and body, feeling for injuries. "Now make her walk away from me, Kate," she said. "And then make her trot. I need to see if she's lame."

Ellie held her breath, hardly daring to look. This was the real test. This would show if Angel had hurt herself badly.

The foal stepped forward cautiously, as if she wasn't sure she could move without pain. But her confidence grew with each step. Soon, she was walking normally, putting her weight evenly on each leg. When Kate asked her to trot, she managed that easily without any sign of limping.

"Thank goodness for that," said Meg. "She's been a very silly pony but there's no harm done. She's escaped with nothing more than a few small cuts."

"That's amazing," said John.

"It's wonderful," said Kate, as she hugged
Angel with delight.

Ellie just grinned. She'd done enough
talking for a while.

Meg pulled her first-aid kit from Kate's
backpack and started dressing Angel's

wounds. Kate held the foal still and John and Ellie acted as assistants, passing the cotton wool and antiseptic powder when Meg wanted it.

Eventually, Meg straightened up and smiled. "She'll be fine now. I'm so glad everything's turned out well in the end.

"Not quite everything," said John. "We still haven't found the—"

Kate kicked him on the ankle before he could finish. "That's supposed to be a secret," she hissed.

"What is?" laughed Meg. "I love secrets, and I'm very good at keeping them. You should know that by now."

"That's true," said Ellie. "So I suppose it doesn't matter if you know about the treasure."

"Especially as we don't know where it is,"
said Kate.

Ellie laughed. "I think I do," she said.

Chapter 10

Everyone stared at Ellie. "How come you know more than us?" asked Kate.

"Because I spotted the site of the old bridge while I was waiting with Angel," explained Ellie. She pointed towards the strange mounds beside the stream. "It's just over there, which means these three oaks are in exactly the right place."

"Brilliant!" yelled John, pulling his metal detector out of his backpack. "I'm all ready. Let's go."

Meg held Angel while Ellie, Kate and John found the oak tree closest to the palace. Just as before, John used his compass to find which way was west. Just as before, they all walked forward ten paces and, just as before, they all ended up in different places.

John pulled out his metal detector, unfolded the super deluxe handle and started to search. Ellie watched him anxiously. Her fists were clenched so tightly that her fingernails dug into the palms of her hands.

Suddenly, the metal detector started to bleep loudly. "Here's the spot," yelled John. "And the signal's really strong. Whatever's down there is much bigger than anything we've found before."

Ellie and Kate grabbed the spades and started to dig. Soon there was a pile of soil beside them and a large hole half a metre deep. "Are you sure this is the right place?" said Ellie, as she paused for a rest.

"Of course I am," said John. "I'll show you." He put the metal detector into the hole and it bleeped even louder than before.

The sound gave Ellie hope. She thrust her spade into the bottom of the hole as hard as she could and hit something solid. With a squeal of delight, she started to scrape away the soil to see what it was.

Kate helped and so did John. This time they didn't find a bottle top or a horseshoe nail. They uncovered a metal box.

John helped Ellie lift it out and put it on

the grass. "Look at that rust," he said. "It's been under the ground for ages."

"A hundred years, we hope," said Ellie.

"Shall I open it?" said John.

"No," said Kate. "Let Ellie do it. She found the map and she found the right place."

Ellie kneeled down in front of the box, while everyone else crowded round to watch.

Princess Ellie's Treasure Hunt

Her stomach was churning with nerves. She couldn't bear the thought of another disappointment. Hardly daring to breathe, she swung the lid open and peered inside.

At the bottom of the box lay a strange collection of objects. There was a painting in a fancy frame, a horseshoe, a plait of long grey hair, a letter, and something wrapped in red cloth.

Kate was bouncing with excitement. "What does the letter say?"

"Is it from a pirate?" asked John.

Ellie picked up the paper and unfolded it. The handwriting was the same as on the map. "Congratulations," she read out. "You have found my treasure. My name is Princess Marissa and I buried this box on my tenth birthday. I love my pony, Tinkerbelle,

The Pony-Mad Princess

more than anything else in the whole world so most of the things I treasure are to do with her. The horseshoe is hers, the plait is made from hairs from her tail and the painting shows how beautiful she is."

Ellie stopped reading and picked up the picture. It showed a girl riding side-saddle on a grey pony.

"Tinkerbelle looks just like Rainbow," said Meg.

"And Marissa looks like the princess in that painting in the tower," said John. "I wonder if that's a picture of her."

Princess Ellie's Treasure Hunt

"This painting's much better than that one," said Kate. "I think it's gorgeous."

"Then you can have it," said Ellie, pushing into her hands. "We've all found the treasure so we ought to share it out."

"That sounds fair," said John. "Now go on with the letter."

Ellie started reading aloud again. "My brother, James, helped me dig the hole and bury the treasure. He's put in the penknife he was given for Christmas."

"It's not there," said John, in a disappointed voice.

"Yes, it is," said Meg. "I can just see the end sticking out from under that red cloth."

John reached into the box and pulled out the penknife. A line of tiny diamonds spelled out a letter J on the polished wood handle.

"I told you there'd be jewels," laughed Ellie.

"J for James and J for John," said Kate. "That's definitely for you to keep."

Ellie agreed. Then she read out the last part of the letter. "There is one other thing here that is not Tinkerbelle's. Unwrap the cloth to find out what it is."

"Go on, Ellie," said John.

"We've both got something already," said Kate. "Whatever's in there must be for you."

Ellie picked up the mysterious bundle and unwrapped it carefully. As the red cloth fell away, the sunlight glittered on a beautiful tiara decorated with golden horseshoes.

"It's the one from the painting," gasped Ellie.

"I told you there'd be gold," laughed John.

Princess Ellie's Treasure Hunt

"And I told you that princess was pony-mad," said Kate.

Meg took the tiara and placed it gently on Ellie's curly hair. "That couldn't be better," she said. "It's a present from one pony-mad princess to another."

John pulled a camera from his backpack. "We ought to have a photo of us all with the treasure," he said.

"I'll take it," said Meg.

"We must include Angel," said Ellie. "We might never have found it without her."

They all crowded round the foal with the treasure box on the ground in front of them.

The Pony-Mad Princess

"Smile," said Meg and she pressed the button.

"Brilliant!" said Ellie. "That photo's going to be the first thing I put in my own treasure box. Maybe another pony-mad princess will find it a hundred years from now."

Pony-Mad Fun & Facts

Parts of a pony

Some of the different parts of a pony have pretty strange names – did you know that there's a part called the "frog", or that ponies have "chestnuts" on their legs? Here's a handy guide...

The top of the pony's head is called the **POLL**.

The joint just above the hoof is called the **FETLOCK**.

On the front leg, the joint above the fetlock is called the **KNEE**.

On the back leg, the joint above the fetlock is called the **HOCK**.

The place where the neck meets the back is called the **WITHERS**.

The long hair on the pony's neck is called the **MANE**.

The part of the mane that hangs down between the pony's ears is called the **FORELOCK**.

The hard part of the hoof is called the **WALL**.

The soft part on the underneath of the foot is called the **FROG**.

Every pony has a small hard lump on the inside of each leg. These are called **CHESTNUTS**.

Princess Ellie's Pony-Mad Quiz

Do you know your **riding hat** from your **reins**? Do you know what colour **Sundance** is? Test your knowledge of Princess Ellie's world with this quiz!

1. Where did Ellie find the treasure map?
a) The library
b) The stables
c) Her bedroom

2. The place where a pony's neck joins his back is called:
a) The dithers
b) The scissors
c) The withers

3. How many oak trees were mentioned on the map?
a) 3
b) 4
c) 5

4. Metal horseshoes are held on with:

a) Glue

b) Nails

c) Screws

5. The person who puts shoes on a horse is called:

a) A farrier

b) A saddler

c) A cobbler

6. A hackamore is:

a) A pony that wants to be ridden more often

b) A bitless bridle

c) A long ride in the country

7. Princess Marissa's golden tiara was decorated with:

a) Diamonds

b) Horseshoes

c) Rubies

Turn the page to
find out the answers...

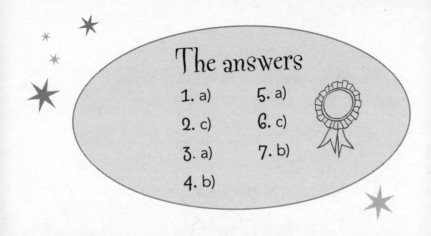

The answers

1. a)   5. a)

2. c)   6. c)

3. a)   7. b)

4. b)

1-3
A good try.

4-6
Great knowledge and a big rosette!

7
You are totally pony-mad –
it's a **gold cup**
for you!

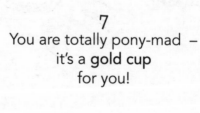

Did you know...?
All about ponies' teeth

Princess Ellie knows that to care for ponies properly, it's important to learn about every part of them! Here are her fantastic facts about ponies' teeth:

* There's a gap between a pony's front and back teeth where there are no teeth at all. This is where the bit sits when you are riding.

* Ponies need to have their teeth checked once or twice a year by a vet, who will use a rasp to smooth down any rough edges and make sure there aren't any other problems.

* Very old horses sometimes find it difficult to eat hay because their teeth are worn out. They need softer food instead.

* An expert can tell a pony's age just by looking at their teeth.

Read on for a sneak preview of
Princess Ellie's next adventure...

Chapter 1

"Go on, boy," urged Princess Ellie, as she cantered Sundance across the palace paddock. The jumping lesson was nearly over. This was her last try at the course, and she was determined to go clear.

She headed Sundance towards the first fence. The chestnut pony responded willingly and cleared the two crossed poles with space to spare.

Ellie felt a surge of excitement – she loved jumping. But she knew she mustn't let her attention slip so she pushed away all her other thoughts and focused on the next fence: a single horizontal pole.

Sundance bounded over that just as easily and, as soon as they landed, Ellie turned him to the right and headed for the next jump. It was another single pole but this time the space underneath was filled with a piece of wood painted with bright red and yellow stripes.

Sundance snorted when he saw it, and Ellie felt him slow slightly and try to swing to the right. She pressed her legs against his sides to urge him onwards and managed to keep him going straight towards the fence. Sundance snorted again when he reached it and jumped much higher than Ellie expected.

He flew over the pole and landed so hard that he almost jolted Ellie out of the saddle. But she kept her balance and turned him left towards the last fence.

It was a double jump: two cross-pole fences set very close together. As Sundance approached the first fence, Ellie concentrated on the vital space between that one and the next. Should she try to get Sundance to cover it in two strides and risk being too far away from the second half of the double or should she let him take three and risk being too close?

She made her decision as Sundance cleared the first fence. She lined him up to the second half and counted his strides, "One, two, three." Then Sundance took off and for a moment, she thought he'd cleared that fence too. But as he landed, he clipped one of the poles with a hind foot, and it fell to the ground.

"Bad luck," called her best friend, Kate, who was sitting in the saddle of a grey pony. "That's exactly what Rainbow did with me."

"Never mind," said Meg, the palace groom, as she walked over to them. "You both did very well. Doubles are tricky. You just need a bit more practice with them."

"Could we try jumping against the clock next time?" asked Ellie. "It looks like fun when I watch riders do that on TV."

"It looks scary too," said Kate. "But I've got to learn to do it if I'm going to ride in the Olympics one day."

Meg laughed. "So that's your plan, is it?" She glanced at Ellie. "And what about you? Are you heading for international competition too?"

"I'd love to," said Ellie. Then she shook her head and sighed. "But Dad won't let me go in for any horse shows, even local ones. He says loads of reporters would turn up to take pictures of me and spoil the show for everyone else. And the flashes on their cameras might frighten the ponies and cause an accident."

"I suppose he's got a point," said Meg. She gave Ellie a sympathetic smile and added, "Being a princess has some drawbacks."

"Maybe I should be glad I'm not royal," said Kate. She reached forward and stroked the grey pony's neck. "But there are some good bits to being a princess. And Rainbow is definitely one of them."

"So is Sundance," Ellie agreed with a grin. "And Starlight and Moonbeam and Shadow."

"I think that's enough jumping for today," said Meg. "The ponies are getting tired." She turned and headed towards the stables, leaving Ellie and Kate to ride back together.

As they walked their ponies side by side, Kate looked at her watch. "Mum and Dad should be back by now. I'm dying to know where they've been today."

"Didn't they tell you?" asked Ellie.

Kate shook her head. "They were very secretive about it. But they said they might come back with some exciting news."

 To find out what happens next read

Princess Ellie's Perfect Plan

Princess Ellie to the Rescue
ISBN: 9781409565963
Can Ellie save her beloved pony, Sundance, when he goes missing?

Princess Ellie's Secret
ISBN: 9781409565970
Ellie comes up with a secret plan to stop Shadow from being sold.

A Puzzle for Princess Ellie
ISBN: 9781409565987
Why won't Rainbow go down the spooky woodland path?

Princess Ellie's Starlight Adventure
ISBN: 9781409565994
Hoofprints appear on the palace lawn and Ellie has to find the culprit.

Princess Ellie's Moonlight Mystery
ISBN: 9781409566007
Ellie is enjoying pony camp, until she hears noises in the night.

A Surprise for Princess Ellie
ISBN: 9781409566014
Ellie sets off in search of adventure, but ends up with a big surprise.

Princess Ellie's Holiday Adventure
ISBN: 9781409566021
Ellie and Kate go to visit Prince John, and get lost in the snow!

Princess Ellie and the Palace Plot
ISBN: 9781409566038
Can Ellie's pony, Starlight, help her uncover the palace plot?

Princess Ellie's Christmas
ISBN: 9781409566045
Ellie's plan for the perfect Christmas present goes horribly wrong...

Princess Ellie Saves the Day
ISBN: 9781409566052
Can Ellie save the day when one of her ponies gets ill?

Princess Ellie's Summer Holiday
ISBN: 9781409566069
Wilfred the Wonder Dog is missing and it's up to Ellie to find him.

Princess Ellie's Treasure Hunt
ISBN: 9781409566076
Will Ellie find the secret treasure buried in the palace grounds?

Princess Ellie's Perfect Plan
ISBN: 9781409556787
Can Ellie find the perfect plan to stop her best friend from leaving?